JP
PET

Don't

For Oscar. You were a good boy. —D.P.

For Steph, who would never eat
(or be in the general vicinity of) a bee. —M.B.

Visit us on the Web! rhcbooks.com

Educators and librarians, for a variety of teaching tools, visit us at RHTeachersLibrarians.com

Library of Congress Cataloging-in-Publication Data
Names: Petty, Dev, author. | Boldt, Mike, illustrator.
Title: Don't eat bees : life lessons from Chip the dog / by Dev Petty ;
illustrated by Mike Boldt.
Description: First edition. | New York : Doubleday, an imprint of Random House Children's Books, [2022] |
Audience: Ages 3–6 | Summary: "Chip the dog shares the wisdom of his seven fruitful years of eating things
he shouldn't." —Provided by publisher.
Identifiers: LCCN 2021020140 (print) | LCCN 2021020141 (ebook) | ISBN 978-0-593-43312-6 (hardcover) |
ISBN 978-0-593-43313-3 (library binding) | ISBN 978-0-593-43314-0 (ebook)
Subjects: CYAC: Eating habits—Fiction. | Dogs—Fiction. | Humorous stories. | LCGFT: Picture books.
Classification: LCC PZ7.P448138 Do 2022 (print) | LCC PZ7.P448138 (ebook) |
DDC [E]—dc23

MANUFACTURED IN CHINA
10 9 8 7 6 5 4 3 2 1
First Edition

Eat Bees

(Life Lessons from Chip the Dog)

written by
Dev Petty

illustrated by
Mike Boldt

DOUBLEDAY BOOKS FOR YOUNG READERS

I am a smart dog.
I am only 7, but that is practically
50 in person years, so I already know
several important dog things.

Like how **cats** are awfully self-important for animals who <u>**poop**</u> in a box.

I know you can dig one **big** hole
and put **30** bones in it...

or

dig **30** holes and put a bone in each.

Another thing I know? Somehow these are all dogs. Yes, **all** of them. Even that one.

But most of my vast knowledge involves what to eat and what not to eat. I will share what I know.

Do: Eat socks.

That is why they come in pairs! There's a spare one just for you.

Like the ones the small persons work on when they finally come home after forever.

Pro Tip 🐾: If you eat them, your small persons will have to stay home to make new important papers.

But...

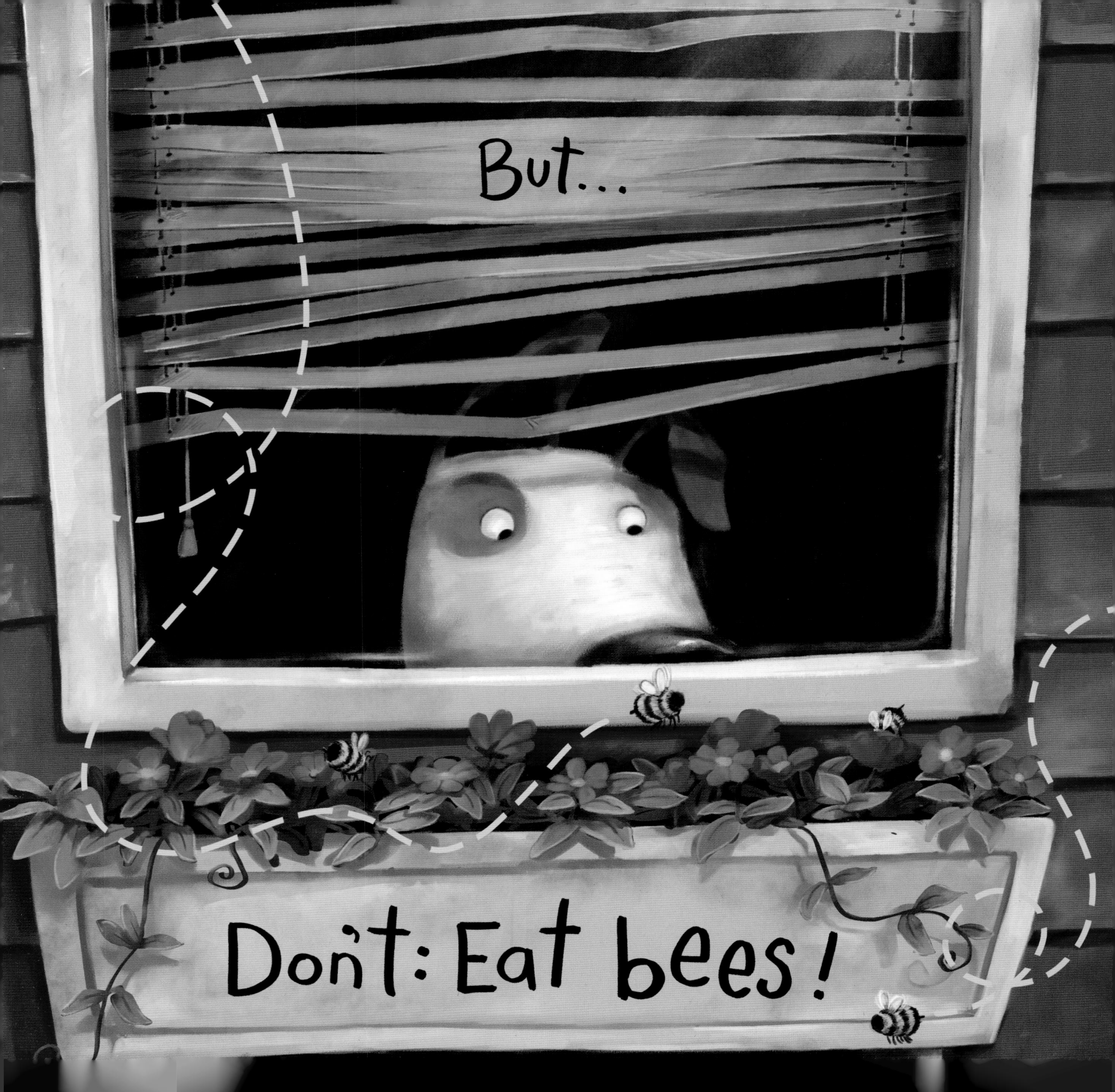

DO: Eat the giant bird they cook at Thanksgiving. Grab what you can and run. It's a fun game.
And you deserve a little fun.
Remember all those papers you ate.

Bees?

No.

DO: Eat Grandpa's teeth.
It will make Grandpa smile, and that, my friend, will make everyone smile. (BUT don't eat bees.)

This will make them love you, and they will scratch that special itchy spot you can't reach.

Yes peas, no bees.

Eat the car.

Eat plants.

Eat dirt (comes with plants).

Eat shoes.

Eat the couch (it had it coming).

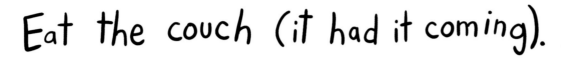

Eat the mail.

For sure, eat the sandwich—
it was obviously for you,
since it had all your
favorite stuff in it.

Don't eat lemons.

Or fire.

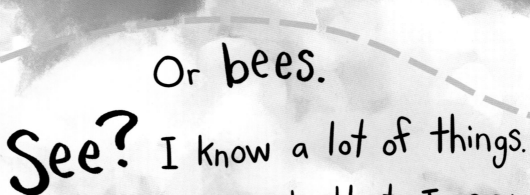

Or bees.

See? I know a lot of things. I am so smart that I can tell you I would never, **ever** do something as silly as eating a bee.

No sir!

Never...

ever...

ever...

...again.

But cactuses? Mittens has been telling me good things about cactuses.